The Great Pirate Adventure

by Mary Māden

™

#7 In A Series

© 1999 by Mary Māden. All rights reserved.
Published in the USA by Dog and Pony Publishing
P.O. Box 3540, Kill Devil Hills, NC 27948
Phone: 252-261-6905
ISBN 1-890479-56-X

*I*t was a beautiful day at the beach. Petey the wild pony and his best friend Tazz the dog were having a great time. They were playing one of their favorite games—pirates!

"*A*rrghh, Matey...take that and that!" yelled Tazz, waving his pirate sword in the air.
"I'm not afraid of you, you scurvy dog!" replied Petey.
"Hey, who are you calling 'scurvy'!" whined Tazz. "I just had a bath last week!"
"Sorry. It was just pirate talk," apologized Petey. "I don't think it means dirty anyway."
"All right then...," said Tazz.
"I have an idea," suggested Petey. "Let's look for buried treasure!"
"For sure," agreed Tazz. "Maybe we can find some real pirate gold!"

$\mathcal{P}$etey and Tazz began to dig in the sand for treasure.
  "I wonder what it was like to be on a real pirate ship," imagined Petey.
"Quit daydreaming and keep digging!" complained Tazz.
Petey noticed something round and white. Whatever it was gleamed in the sand.
"I found something!" yelled Petey.
"We're rich!" shouted Tazz as he ran over to see what Petey had found.
"Mustn't touch!" said an ancient but gentle voice.

Suprised, Petey and Tazz looked around. They saw a great old sea turtle.

"Those are turtle eggs," explained old Grandmother Turtle. "One must not touch or disturb turtle eggs."

"Yes, Ma'am!" said Petey and Tazz.

"Since you are such good boys," said Grandmother Turtle, "I will tell you a story—a tale of a brave adventurer named Mort. Mort sailed on some of the most famous pirate ships of all time!"

"I've never heard of Mort," said Petey. "Who was he?"

"You never heard of Mort!" cried Grandmother Turtle. "Why Mortimer T. Tortuga, or Mort for short, was just the most famous turtle in all of turtle history!"

"Mort sailed on pirate ships from the Caribbean to New England," continued Grandmother Turtle. "He had some exciting adventures!"
"Wow!" said Petey. "Tell us more!"
"I'll tell you a tale of one of Mort's most thrilling adventures," said Grandmother Turtle.

It was a long time ago when pirates sailed the seas, and it happened something like this...

ort blinked his eyes trying to see. It was dark! Mort kicked his feet in the air. He was flat on his back! Mort wiggled and squirmed. It was no use!

Mort couldn't flip himself over.

"Oh dear!" moaned Mort. "Where am I? What's to become of me?"

"You're in the hold of a pirate ship, Matey," said a voice, "and you're about to become turtle soup!"

"What?" said Mort. "Who's there? Where are you?"
Someone struck a match. Mort stared in amazement. There stood a monkey wearing an eye patch!
"Me name's Chee Chee," answered the monkey, "and I'm a pirate!"
Suddenly, Mort and Chee Chee heard shouting and angry cries coming from the deck above them.

"Shiver me timbers! They be after me!" wailed Chee Chee.
   "Who's after you?" asked Mort.
"Sssh! They'll hear you," warned Chee Chee. "Pirates! They be after me!"
"But, I thought you were a pirate," said Mort, confused.
"And that I am!" said Chee Chee proudly. "I'm the smartest pirate of
all. I steal treasure from other pirates. And these," Chee Chee
pointed up, "they be wanting their treasure back!"
The noise above them grew louder.

"*H*ow would you like me to flip you over on your feet?" offered Chee Chee.

"Oh please," cried Mort. "I hate being upside down!"

"I'll flip you upright if you'll hide this for me," Chee Chee handed Mort a sack. "Put this in your shell until I ask you for it."

Chee Chee pushed and pulled Mort. He tugged and shoved until the turtle was back on his feet.

"Arrghh...you be a fat one!" said Chee Chee, out of breath. "Hark! I hear 'em coming down...I best be trying to hide topside!"

Chee Chee disappeared through the trapdoor of the hold. Mort sat all alone in the darkness.

"here he is!" yelled the pirate captain Vane. "Grab him Mates!"
The pirates chased Chee Chee all over the deck of the ship. But try as they might,
the pirates couldn't catch the little monkey!
"Blast you!" roared Captain Vane, "I'll cut you to ribbons when I catch you!"
Out of the corner of his eye, Chee Chee saw Mort climb out of the hold. None of the pirates
saw the turtle. They were too busy chasing Chee Chee! Quietly, Mort slipped over the side.

"Hey!" yelled Chee Chee, "come back here with me treasure!" Chee Chee ran over to the ship's rail and shouted down at Mort, "Come back you ungrateful turtle!"
Too late, Chee Chee realized he had forgotten all about the pirates! They were behind him waving their big pirate swords! Chee Chee was trapped. The little monkey knew there was only one way to escape... Chee Chee held his nose. "I hates water!" he yelled as he jumped overboard.
"Let him go!" ordered the pirate captain. "Let the sharks have him!"

Chee Chee landed right on top of Mort! "Ouch!" cried Mort. "Get off of me!"
"I can't!" said Chee Chee. "I can't swim!"
"Hold on then," said Mort, "I'll keep you afloat."
"Where's me treasure?" asked Chee Chee, feeling under Mort's shell. "It's not here!"
"It must have fallen into the water," said Mort. "We'll never find it now."
"What a day," groaned Chee Chee. "Me treasure's gone, and here I am sitting on a turtle's back in the middle of the ocean!"
"It could be worse," said Mort. "At least we are alive."
"What are we going to do now?" Chee Chee whined. "There's nothing but miles and miles of water!"
"You can catch a ride on the next ship we see," answered Mort. "As for me, I'm home. I live in the ocean."
"Lucky you!" snapped the grumpy little monkey.

*H*ours and hours passed with no sign of a ship. Suddenly, several ships appeared on the horizon.

"Here! Over here!" shouted Chee Chee, standing on Mort's back and waving his arms.

"There be a strange sight," said the captain of the biggest ship. "Fetch them up and let's take a look."

Chee Chee and Mort were pulled aboard and dumped at the captain's feet.

"Major, come look at this!" roared the captain with laughter. "This sight would amuse even you!"

Another man dressed in fine clothes joined the captain.

"Shiver me timbers!" cried Chee Chee. "It's Blackbeard and Stede Bonnet!"

"Who are they?" whispered Mort.

"Pirates!" gasped Chee Chee.

The pirates threw Mort and Chee Chee down below into the dark hold.

"Ouch!" howled Chee Chee, landing on his head.

"Oh, woe is me!" cried Mort in fear.

"You should be scared," said a voice. "Blackbeard's one mean pirate!"

"He's feared from the Spanish Main to Philadelphia town," said another voice.

"He just took the whole harbor of Charleston hostage!" said yet another voice.

"Me thinks we have company," said Chee Chee, striking a match, "let me put some light on the subject... there now... well blow me down!"

All around Chee Chee were turtles!

"What happened in Charleston?" Chee Chee asked the turtles.
  "Blackbeard, Bonnet and over 300 pirates sailed into the harbor.
They took some ships and the people on them prisoner.
Blackbeard said he would kill the people if he didn't get a chest
of medicine. The whole town was terrified!"
"Did Blackbeard kill the people?" whispered Mort.
  "No, he let them go," answered the turtle. "They gave
Blackbeard the medicine, and he sailed away."
  "But, not before he robbed everyone of their valuables!" added
another turtle.

"So where are we now?" asked Chee Chee.

"We're on Blackbeard's pirate ship, Queen Anne's Revenge," answered one of the turtles, "and we're headed north to Beaufort in North Carolina."

"We heard Blackbeard and some of his men talking," added another turtle, "Blackbeard wants to keep the treasure for himself. He plans to split up the crew and get rid of most of them including that gentleman pirate, Stede Bonnet!"

"How does Blackbeard plan to do that?" asked Mort.

"By running the Queen Anne's Revenge aground!" answered the turtles.

"We have to get out of here!" cried Chee Chee.

"First we need to get everyone back up on their feet!" said Mort. Chee Chee and Mort helped all the turtles flip upright. Just then, the ship came to a grinding stop! With a loud crack, the Queen Anne's Revenge ran aground!

"We've struck ground!" cried Chee Chee.

"Let's get off this ship!" said Mort. Mort and Chee Chee climbed out of the hold. Right in front of them was Blackbeard! The fierce pirate was yelling and giving orders. "Follow us!" Mort instructed the turtles. Quietly, Mort, Chee Chee, and the turtles crept behind Blackbeard. Carefully they slipped overboard. The turtles swam quickly away from the pirates.

Chee Chee rode on Mort's back.

"Whew! That was close!" cried the little monkey, holding on for dear life.

"I don't ever want to see another pirate as long as I live!" declared Mort.

ort headed south to warmer waters. Chee Chee sat perched on top of his shell.
"Can't you swim any faster?" complained Chee Chee, "I'll never see dry land at this rate!"
"Sorry," said Mort, adding under his breath, "I have a good mind to give you a flip."
"What did you say?" asked Chee Chee.
"I see a ship," fibbed Mort.
The ship came along side them. Chee Chee laid flat against Mort's shell. "Are they pirates?"
whispered the little monkey, fearfully.
"I see two women on board," answered Mort. "So they must not be pirates."
The women on the ship threw a rope over the side.
"I'm saved!" yelled Chee Chee, standing on Mort's back and
waving his arms.

hee Chee climbed aboard. "Me thanks to you kind ladies," said the little monkey, bowing and tipping his hat. Chee Chee noticed something different about these ladies. They were dressed like men ... and they carried big swords! Chee Chee saw a man dressed in bright calico pants. It was the pirate captain, Calico Jack Rackham! The women were Anne Bonny and Mary Read — the meanest women pirates in all of the Caribbean!

"Shiver me timbers — more pirates!" screamed Chee Chee.

Chee Chee ran to the back of the ship and looked over the rail. Mort was swimming away. "Wait, Mort," called Chee Chee, "wait for me!" The little monkey dove straight into the water!

With a big loud splash, Chee Chee hit the water. Down the little monkey sank. Mort heard the noise and turned around. He saw his friend vanish beneath the waves.

Quickly, Mort dove under the water. Mort swam under the monkey. With all his might, Mort pushed Chee Chee to the surface. "Are you okay? Chee Chee!" cried Mort. "Speak to me, little buddy!" Chee Chee's eyes fluttered open. "I hates water," groaned the little monkey.

"And that's the end of the story," said Grandmother Turtle. "Mort carried Chee Chee back to the jungles of Costa Rica. The little monkey gave up the pirating life and lived happily ever after. The pirates all came to a bad end. And as for Mort...well, Mort went on to become the most famous turtle in all of turtle history!"

"Wow!" said Petey. "Mort sure met a lot of pirates. He had one great pirate adventure!"

"For sure," agreed Tazz.

Petey and Tazz thanked Grandmother Turtle for her story.

"Grandmother Turtle's story sure was an adventure!" said Petey.
"Sure enough," agreed Tazz. "But, time's awastin', Petey my boy!"
"Let's go!" shouted Petey, galloping away.

Side by side, their eyes shining with excitement, Petey and Tazz start out on their next big adventure!

Pirate Facts (a hidden treasure of information)

In days gone by, pirates roamed the seas. A pirate robs ships at sea. A captured ship is called a "prize." Television and movies often show the life of a pirate as exciting and glamorous. But a pirate's life was a hard life! It could get boring sailing around just waiting for a ship. Being a pirate was dangerous too. If you were caught being a pirate—you were hanged! And as for treasure... well sometimes pirates did get lucky and take a rich ship. (It's not true that pirates buried their treasure—they usually spent it as fast as they could!)

The food on a pirate's ship could be terrible! Pirates mostly ate "hard tack" (hard, dry biscuits). And if you wanted to wash your hard tack down with water... well the water was usually stale and awful. Pirates carried limes to prevent scurvy. (Scurvy is a disease caused by not having enough vitamin C.) Scurvy makes your hair and teeth fall out! Pirates also carried chickens and other animals on board for fresh food. But the main source of fresh meat was turtles! Pirates just loved turtle soup!

SOME FAMOUS PIRATES...

Blackbeard
(alias Edward Teach or Thatch)

Blackbeard was called the *"fiercest pirate of them all."* There aren't many real facts known about *Blackbeard*—but many legends have sprung up about him. He was probably born in England. He roamed America's Atlantic Coast and the Caribbean from 1716-1718. He was killed and beheaded off Ocracoke Island, NC on November 22, 1718. Experts think they found his famous ship, *Queen Anne's Revenge*, at Beaufort, NC.

Stede Bonnet
(the "gentleman pirate")

Stede Bonnet was a plantation owner in Barbados. It is said he became a pirate to get away from his nagging wife. *Bonnet* bought a ship and went to sea. He sailed on the Atlantic Coast and the Caribbean. He met up with *Blackbeard* and agreed to sail with him. *Blackbeard* took over Bonnet's ship. *Bonnet* became a *"guest"* aboard Blackbeard's ship, *Queen Anne's Revenge*. (*Bonnet* was really being held against his will.) *Blackbeard* and *Bonnet* parted ways after *Blackbeard* ran the *Queen Anne's Revenge* aground. (*Blackbeard* also took all the treasure!) *Bonnet* was caught near Cape Fear, NC.

He was hanged in Charleston, SC in 1718.

Anne Bonny

Anne Bonny grew up in the Carolinas. She married a sailor named *James Bonny* and moved to the Bahamas. Anne and her husband didn't get along. She met a pirate captain by the name of John *"Calico Jack" Rackham*. Anne ran away with *"Calico Jack"* and became a pirate too. She dressed in men's clothes. She was as fierce a pirate as any man! She was captured along with another woman pirate, *Mary Read*, and *"Calico Jack"* in 1720. They were all taken to jail. (*Rackham* was hanged.) *Anne Bonny* and *Mary Read* were not hanged because they were both going to have babies! There are no records of what happened to *Anne Bonny*. Legend has it that her father paid to get her out of jail, and she raised her baby as a free woman.

Mary Read

Mary Read had an unusual childhood. Her mother dressed her in boy's clothes and passed her off as a boy. *Mary Read* served as a soldier and a sailor. She lived most of her life as a man. She was on a ship taken by *"Calico Jack" Rackham*. Not knowing she was a woman, *Rackham* took her on as part of his crew. *Anne Bonny* and *Mary Read* became good friends. *Rackham*, thinking *Mary* was a man, became jealous. *Anne* and *Mary* had to tell him that *Mary* was really a woman. So, now *Rackham* had two woman pirates as part of his crew! *Mary Read* was arrested and jailed along with *Rackham* and *Anne Bonny* in 1720. She became sick and died in jail.